A Different Kind of Passover

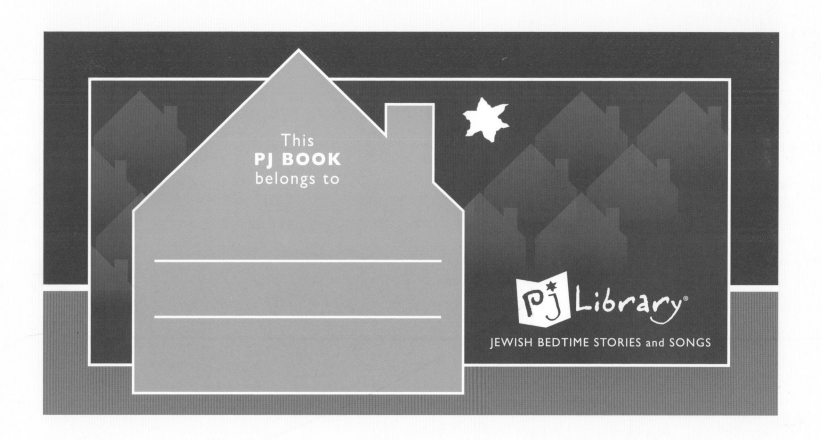

This **PJ BOOK** belongs to

_____

_____

PJ Library®

JEWISH BEDTIME STORIES and SONGS

For Leila and Eli, the great-great grandchildren of the
Grandma and Grandpa in this story – L.L.S.

KAR-BEN PUBLISHING
A division of Lerner Publishing Group, Inc.
241 First Avenue North
Minneapolis, MN 55401 USA
1-800-4-Karben

Website address: www.karben.com

Main body text set in Zemestro Std 15/20.
Typeface provided by Monotype Typography.

Library of Congress Cataloging-in-Publication Data

Names: Strauss, Linda Leopold, author. | Tugeau, Jeremy, illustrator.
Title: A different kind of Passover / by Linda Leopold-Strauss ; illustrated by
    Jeremy Tugeau.
Description: Minneapolis : Kar-Ben Publishing, [2017] | Summary: "Passover at
    Grandma and Grandpa's house is a little different this year because Grandpa
    just got out of the hospital. But with a little help from Jessica and her family,
    Grandpa is still able to take part in the seder"— Provided by publisher.
Identifiers: LCCN 2016009542 (print) | LCCN 2016029188 (ebook) | ISBN
    9781512400977 (lb : alk. paper) | ISBN 9781512401028 (pb : alk. paper) | ISBN
    9781512427233 (eb pdf)
Subjects: | CYAC: Passover—Fiction. | Judaism—Customs and practices—Fiction. |
    Family life—Fiction. | Grandfathers—Fiction.
Classification: LCC PZ7.S91245 Di 2017 (print) | LCC PZ7.S91245 (ebook) | DDC [E]—
    dc23

LC record available at https://lccn.loc.gov/2016009542

Manufactured in China
1-38933-20907-6/6/2016

031727.8K1/B0971/A6

A Different Kind of Passover

Linda Leopold Strauss

illustrated by **Jeremy Tugeau**

KAR-BEN
PUBLISHING

"*Mah nishtanah halailah hazeh mikol haleilot?* Why is this night different from all other nights?"

Five times, ten times, all the way to Grandma and Grandpa's, I practice the Four Questions. At our seder tomorrow it will be my job to ask the questions, and Grandpa will answer by telling us the story of Passover.

But then I remember that Grandpa was in the hospital until yesterday, so maybe he won't be at the seder. Mom says he's better, but still very weak.

I can't imagine our seder without Grandpa at the table. Even though seder night is supposed to be different from all other nights, what I love most about Passover at my grandparents' are the things that are always the same.

Like . . .

Running up the stairs to the apartment after Grandma buzzes us in.

The family photos on the wall near the piano.

The good smells coming from the kitchen.

The pile of blankets and pillows that my cousins and I use to make beds on the floor. (We always sleep over on seder nights.)

But this year Grandpa isn't at the front door, holding his arms out for a hug. And instead of giving us noisy kisses, Grandma says, "Quiet, everyone! You'll wake up Grandpa!"

"Maybe we should just have a mini-seder this year," Aunt Alice says. "That would make it easier on everyone."

Grandma gives Aunt Alice a look and offers me a spoonful of chicken soup.

"It's perfect, Grandma," I say.

"And you tasted the fish?" Grandma asks Mom. "It's okay?"

"When did you ever make a bad piece of fish?" Mom says, hugging her.

"I'm serious," Aunt Alice persists. "Instead of having the whole seder, Jessica can just ask the Four Questions and we'll have a nice Passover dinner. A little bird told me Jessie's been practicing the questions in Hebrew."

"In Hebrew?" marvels Grandma. "Really, Jessica?"

"Yes. But we need to have the answers, too, Aunt Alice!" I insist. "That's what Grandpa always says. Just ask him!"

"No one's asking Grandpa anything," Aunt Alice says sharply.

Sadly I take out the haggadahs. Will we even be reading the Passover story tonight?

"What about the afikomen?" asks Maddie. "If Grandpa doesn't hide it, how can we look for it?"

My heart hurts. Last year I was the one who found the afikomen, and Grandpa gave me a kiss and a silver dollar to get it back. I want so much for this year to be like last year.

I set down the haggadahs and walk out of the kitchen.

Grandpa gives me a weak smile when I come into his room. "Hi, sweetheart. What's up?"

"Grandma's making matzah ball soup. Can you smell it?"

"I can smell everything. I can hear everything. I just can't get to it," Grandpa says in a grouchy voice.

I stare at him. Grandpa is never grouchy.

He tries to sit up. "Let's have some help with these pillows," he says.

Grandpa looks a lot better after I plump up the pillows behind him. At the seder, he would have leaned on pillows, too, because in ancient days leaning on pillows at meals was a sign of freedom.

"Grandpa!" I exclaim. Suddenly I know how he can come to the seder!

My shout brings Grandma running to the bedroom.

"See how Grandpa's door opens to the dining room?" I say excitedly. "He can lead the seder from his bed!"

"Go to the seder in my pajamas?" says Grandpa, shocked.

"Does God care if you're in your pajamas?" retorts Grandma. "Listen to your smart granddaughter." She hugs me.

We spend the day getting ready for the seder. We take out the velvet matzah cover and put in the three matzahs, including the afikomen. We arrange the seder plate and set the table. We put Elijah's cup in a place of honor.

As I sit at the seder table, these things are the same as always . . .

The beautiful seder plate.

A haggadah at every plate.

Grandpa leading the seder.

Me asking the Four Questions—this year in Hebrew!

The ten drops that I drip from my grape juice glass with my finger, one for each plague God sent the Egyptians until they let our people go.

And Grandma saying (just when my stomach can't wait another minute), "Time to eat!"

These things are different . . .

Grandpa sitting in bed in his pajamas and getting tired halfway through the answers. (Uncle Steven helps him with the rest of the service.)

Mark getting to sip sweet wine instead of grape juice, since he has just had his bar mitzvah.

Daddy forgetting to say Grandma's horseradish is strong enough to clear his sinuses (but Aunt Alice saying it instead).

And this year, of course, Grandpa won't be hiding the afikomen.

As Aunt Alice clears the fish plates, Mom checks on Grandpa. She whispers something to him and fusses with his pillows. I see Grandpa smile. Then his eyes flutter shut. Mom pulls up his blanket and comes back to the table.

After dinner, it's time to finish the seder, but Uncle Steven doesn't have the afikomen. How did it go missing? We need it to finish the seder! Mark, Maddie, and I search all over the house.

We save Grandpa's room for last. When I come near his bed, he opens one eye and winks at me.

Suddenly I remember the smile on his face when Mom went into his room. I check under his pillows—and there is the afikomen!

Uncle Steven gives me a silver dollar in exchange for the afikomen, and I run back to give Grandpa a kiss—just like I did last year.

After we open the door for Elijah, we put down our haggadahs and sing the final Passover songs, our voices mixing—Mark's lower than it used to be, Grandpa's more wobbly.

But the same or different, I know this is what I'll remember next year:
My family on this special night. Together at Passover.